REUBEN "RIVER" REEVES was a Chicago trumpet man who played a "hot" style that spiced up some of the nightlife of that great American city through the 1920s and early 1930s. His chatty, pealing trumpet got folks making silly faces at one another, got their feet moving on the dance floor for sure. (Album: *Reuben Reeves and Omer Simeon*)

"PAPA" JO JONES taught other jazz drummers how to truly swing. Dubbed the "father of the hi-hat" for his crisp, infectious swing on the cymbals, he'd also hit his rims in moments you didn't expect just to make you listen to a part of the tune you hadn't noticed was there. His inventiveness on the drums made him sort of like the first person to throw cinnamon in chili—understated, but oh so sweet. (Album: *The Jo Jones Special*)

BUDDY RICH was nicknamed "super drummer" because he played so fa-furious and with such precision chops, it boggled people's minds. His drum solos are legendary— when he played, the sweat just poured off him—and the big bands he led blew the roof off whatever house they played. Countless drummers who've come and gone have tried to cook like Buddy on the kit. (Album: *Big Swing Face*)

Listening to **"BIG SID" CATLETT** drum is like watching popcorn pop. Now imagine the popcorn machine's also gracefully swing dancing around the room while it pops and you've got a sense of the irresistible joy and magic this great drummer and showman brought to every band he played in. (Album: Louis Armstrong: *The Complete Town Hall Concert 1947*)

ART BLAKEY was the head chef in his own jazz kitchen for decades and decades. King of the drumroll, he could do it all—swing, bop, solo—with force and aplomb. He led an ever-changing group of young musicians called the Jazz Messengers who learned all the prep work before going on to greatness. (Album: *Buhaina's Delight*)

atheneum

ATHENEUM BOOKS FOR YOUNG READERS
An imprint of Simon & Schuster Children's Publishing Division
1230 Avenue of the Americas, New York, New York 10020
Text © 2021 by Jarrett Dapier
Illustrations © 2021 by Eugenia Mello
Book design by Greg Stadnyk © 2021 by Simon & Schuster, Inc.

ATHENEUM BOOKS FOR YOUNG READERS
is a registered trademark of Simon & Schuster, Inc.
Atheneum logo is a trademark of Simon & Schuster, Inc.
For information about special discounts for bulk purchases, please contact
Simon & Schuster Special Sales at 1-866-506-1949 or business@simonandschuster.com.

The Simon & Schuster Speakers Bureau
can bring authors to your live event.
For more information or to book an event,
contact the Simon & Schuster Speakers Bureau
at 1-866-248-3049 or visit our website at
www.simonspeakers.com.

The text for this book was set in Clarendon.
Custom lettering by Yani&Guille.
The illustrations for this book were rendered digitally.
Manufactured in China
0621 SCP

First Edition
2 4 6 8 10 9 7 5 3 1
Library of Congress Cataloging-in-Publication Data
Names: Dapier, Jarrett, author. | Mello, Eugenia, illustrator.
Title: Jazz for lunch! / Jarrett Dapier ; illustrated by Eugenia Mello.
Description: First edition. | New York : Atheneum Books for Young Readers, [2021] |
"A Caitlyn Dlouhy Book." | Audience: Ages 4–8. | Audience: Grades K–1. |
Summary: After lunch at a very crowded jazz cafe, a boy and his Auntie Nina are inspired to create a
feast of their own with such treats as Thelonious Monk fish and Nat King cole slaw.
Identifiers: LCCN 2020007964 | ISBN 9781534454088 (hardcover) | ISBN 9781534454095 (eBook)
Subjects: CYAC: Stories in rhyme. | Jazz—Fiction. | Cooking—Fiction. | Dance—Fiction. | Aunts—Fiction.
Classification: LCC PZ8.3.D2397 Jaz 2021 | DDC [E]—dc23
LC record available at https://lccn.loc.gov/2020007964

For Franny, who made lunch with
me while we listened to jazz
—J. D.

For my grandma, who doesn't cook but
loves music, cannot contain her body
from dancing, and taught me about the
contagious, delicious matter that is joy
—E. M.

JAZZ FOR LUNCH!

Written by **Jarrett Dapier**

Pictures by **Eugenia Mello**

A Caitlyn Dlouhy Book

Atheneum Books for Young Readers

New York London Toronto Sydney New Delhi

STRUTTIN' with my Auntie Nina
down to a CLUB.
We're gonna hear some music
and then eat some GRUB.

Nina's there for lunch
almost every other day.
Musicians hit the stage,
and this is what they play:

JAZZ FOR LUNCH!
The beats got *SOUL!*
JAZZ FOR LUNCH!
Ham on a *ROLL!*
JAZZ FOR LUNCH!
The tunes got *SWING!*
JAZZ FOR LUNCH!
Shout, dance, and *sing!*

PEAL of the trumpet and the **zest** of the hi-hat,
knives go *CHOP*—hear the **SIZZLE** of some bacon fat.
Sounds of the kitchen and the music mix together.
Nina winks at me 'cause we are birds of a feather.

JAZZ FOR LUNCH!
The club's got SOUL!

JAZZ FOR LUNCH!
Eat a

JAZZ FOR LUNCH!
The food's got SWING!

JAZZ FOR LUNCH!
Shout, dance, and sing!

Wanna get up close, but we're stuck in the back.

I can't see the drums, and I can't get a snack.

Dancing dudes and ladies are stomping on my feet,

talking too loud,
and I can't stand
the HEAT.

Nina walks me out 'fore the set is through,

says, "Come by tomorrow, I got a surprise for you.

I think that me and you, we could do *something great.*

After what we just heard, I'm *Fittin'* to **create!**"

The next day at Nina's place
we're both on the make.

"Throw some jazz on
the stereo, for heaven's sake!"
Now we got a rhythm kitchen,
high flyin' STOMP.
TEACHIN' me to cook,
it's a hot house romp!

JAZZ FOR LUNCH!

Playin' food, *steamin'* tunes.

JAZZ FOR LUNCH!

Stirrin' fats, *Lickin'* spoons.

JAZZ FOR LUNCH!

SHAKIN' cinnamon in the chili.

JAZZ FOR LUNCH!

Salt peanuts, gettin' *Silly!*

Bone-in drumstick,
cookin' on the fly,
fresh new dishes,
a jam session high—
Nina's master chef
and I'm her
Shorty Baker,
second banana, junior cook,
boogie-woogie
bootyshaker!

Pit-Pat the peanut butter,
SLAP on the **JELLY,**
sweet potato sweet potato,
Philly Joe BELLY,
pizzicato panna cotta
parmigiana **CHEESE,**
Art Tatum tots
and a hot Reuben **REEVES!**

"Ladies AND Gentlemen, GIRLS AND Boys!
Put your hands together now.
MAKE SOME NOISE!
Like to introduce you
to my nephew junior COOK,
makes a meal of the drums.
Just take a look."

Chikka-ssss
Chikka-ssss
CRASH! FLAM!
Triplet pan!

Chikka-ssss

Chikka-ssss

Jo Jones, drummer man!

SPLASH CYMBAL

guacamole!
Hot Buddy Rich pozole!

Saltshaker TAMBOURINE!
Sid Catlett nectarine!

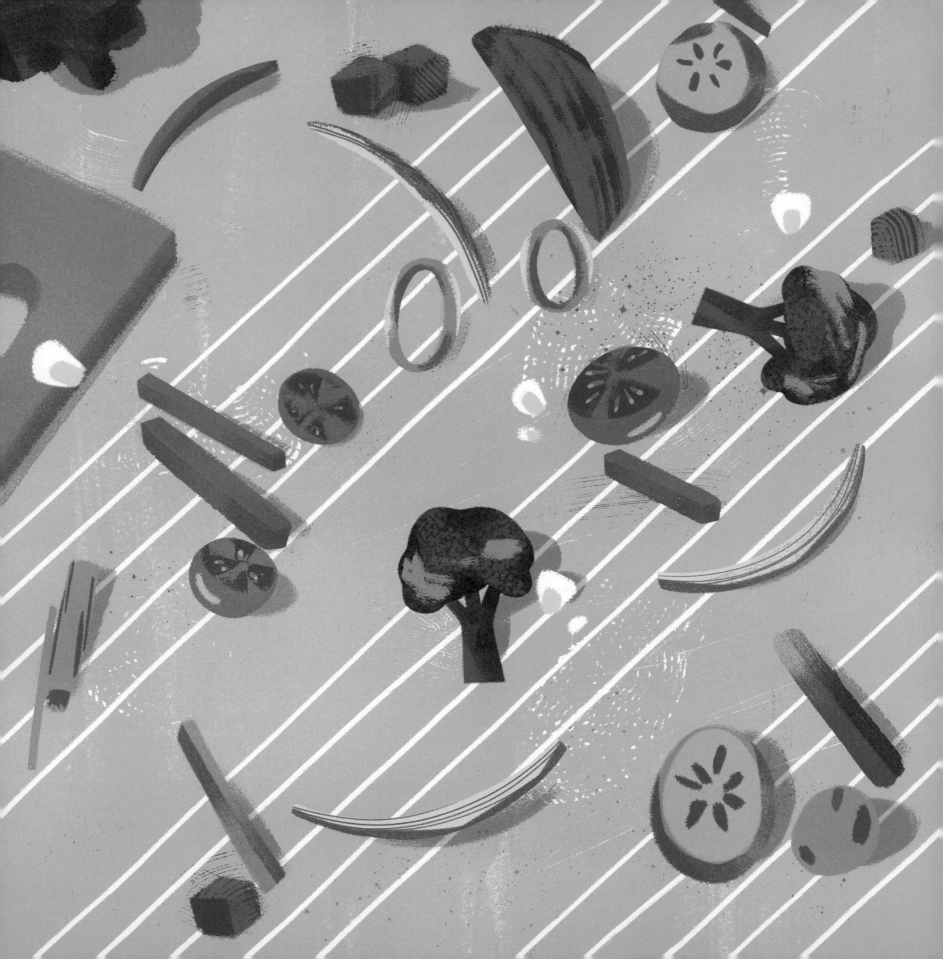

Now I wanna tell you 'bout
the food that we made.
We **SLICED** it and **DICED** it
with the edge of a blade.
We named every dish after
favorite jazz greats.
Now check out those hot eats
upon your plates:

hoppin' *John Coltrane,*

ART PEPPER steak,

Billie Hollandaise sauce,

DEXTER GORDON cheesecake!

JAZZ FOR LUNCH!

Let it cool . . .

Let it cool...

JAZZ FOR LUNCH!

Keep it cool . . .

Keep it cool...

KNOCK KNOCK

"Hey now, Auntie Nina, who's that *knockin'* at the door?"

JAZZ FOR LUNCH!
A rhythm JAMBALAYA!

JAZZ FOR LUNCH!
All-in, bounce HIGHER!

JAZZ FOR LUNCH!
Finger-zinger freak-lip!

JAZZ FOR LUNCH!
Ella Bessie chip dip!

JAZZ FOR LUNCH!
Chomp a trombone— CRUNCH!

JAZZ FOR LUNCH!
Eat a drumroll— munch!

JAZZ FOR LUNCH!
We dance and we eat!

JAZZ FOR LUNCH!
HOT FOOD and FRESH BEATS!

What's for dinner?"

THELONIOUS MONK—This guy was an odd, brilliant duck who could play the piano's keys with ingenious deftness from deep within his heart. One moment he would find what was salty and sweet in ingredients we didn't know were there, and the next he'd be messing around just tinkling bright and goofy like he was playing the song in the back of an ice-cream truck. (Album: *Brilliant Corners*)

NAT KING COLE—This elegant superstar is known for his years as an unforgettable vocalist who crooned buttermilk-biscuit warm orchestral numbers, but first he was a jazz piano man. His singing and playing with the King Cole Trio were all crisp style, playful noodles, winks, and smiles. (Album: Nat King Cole Trio, *The Complete Capitol Transcription Sessions*)

Red Hot Peppers—This jazz band lasted only a handful of years at the end of the 1920s in Chicago, but was led by a great pianist named **JELLY ROLL MORTON** and featured other legendary early jazz musicians with names like Kid Ory and Baby Dodds. Their playing was fast, quick, and "hot"—and they threw it all in the pot. (Album: Jelly Roll Morton, *Birth of the Hot*)

JOHN COLTRANE was raw sugar bopping out of a saxophone: He was sweet, bombastic, and big, but could also be oh so smooth. He was a pot roast, too, made for just me and you. Comfort food. But also experimental seasoning and always with the best groups of jazz-cat cooks backing him up with fire and heart. Coltrane was *the* jazz saxophonist of the twentieth century. (Album: *Giant Steps*)

ART PEPPER—This restless saxophonist could coax the sweetest honey out of his horn in brilliant, flowing melody after melody. His jazz dishes were elegant affairs with every garnish and every accent just right. (Album: *Art Pepper Meets the Rhythm Section*)